A Ghost
a Witch
and a Goblin

A Ghost
a Witch
and a Goblin

Illustrated by ROSALIND FRY

SCHOLASTIC BOOK SERVICES

NEW YORK · TORONTO · LONDON · AUCKLAND · SYDNEY · TOKYO

ISBN: 0-590-04447-8

Copyright © 1970 by Scholastic Magazines, Inc. All rights reserved. Published by Scholastic
Book Services, a division of Scholastic Magazines, Inc.

21 20 19 18 17 16 15 14 13 12   01/8

Printed in the U.S.A.   07

The Ghost Catcher

Now this is a very old story. It is about a young barber who did not really want to be a barber. And it is about a ghost — two ghosts.

The young barber's name was Tom. Tom didn't like being a barber. He didn't like cutting men's hair or shaving their faces. He really wanted to be a farmer.

But Tom's father was a barber. And when Tom's father died, all he left his son was his bag of barber tools — razors, scissors, brushes, combs, and a mirror. So what could Tom do? He tried to be a barber too. In those days, you had to do whatever your father did.

Well, Tom was a clever boy, but he wasn't a good barber. And after a while people stopped coming to him.

"He is not as good a barber as his father," they said.

"I'd rather be a farmer," Tom thought. "But if I have to be a barber, I will leave this town. I will go to the city where no one knows that my father was a better barber than I."

And so Tom picked up his bag of barber tools — razors, scissors, brushes, combs, and a mirror — and set off for the city.

Tom walked all morning and he walked all afternoon.

When night came, Tom sat under a willow tree to rest. The city was still a long way off, and Tom decided to spend the night under the willow tree. "Then I can start out fresh in the morning," he said to himself. Tom lay down on the ground and fell asleep at once.

As luck would have it, that very willow tree was haunted by a ghost.

Soon after Tom fell asleep, the ghost floated down from the treetop crying, "BOOOOOOO!"

Tom woke up at once. "What a bad dream," he said to himself. "I dreamed this willow tree was haunted by a ghost."

"BOOOOOOOO!" cried the ghost again. Now he was right at Tom's ear. This was not a dream! Tom had to think fast.

"Don't you come close to me, ghost," Tom said quickly. "D-Do you know what I am? I-I'm a GHOST CATCHER! That's what I am! I catch ghosts and put them in my ghost bag."

And with that Tom opened his bag of barber tools and pulled up the mirror. "Here, let me show you one ghost I've caught tonight," he said. Tom held the mirror up to the ghost's face. "I think I'll put you in the bag to keep him company."

The ghost looked into the mirror — and what did he see? His own face, of course. But he didn't know that. He thought the barber really did have a ghost in the bag.

"Oh, please," begged the ghost, "don't put me in your ghost bag. I'll give you anything you want. Just let me go."

"Anything I want?" said Tom. "Then I want a bag of gold. Maybe two bags of gold."

Zip! In a wink two bags of gold were at Tom's feet.

"Good enough," Tom said. "I promise not to put you in my bag this time. But remember, if you bother me again, into the ghost bag you go." As soon as Tom let the mirror fall back into the bag, the ghost was gone.

Tom never did go to the city. He took some of the gold the ghost had given him and he bought himself a farm. He bought cows and pigs and horses and chickens. Tom was a fine farmer. He didn't have to cut hair or shave faces anymore. But Tom kept his bag of barber tools — and that was very clever of him.

For, as luck would have it, the ghost met his cousin one day and told him everything that had happened. At the end of his story, the cousin burst out laughing.

"Hoo, hoo, hoo," he laughed. "No man can catch a ghost. And there is no such thing as a ghost bag. You have been tricked."

"Well, go and see for yourself," the ghost said. "But don't blame me if that man puts you in his bag."

The cousin floated over to Tom's house and peeked through the window.

Tom was eating his supper. He felt a cold breeze and looked up. Another ghost! Tom ran to get his bag of tools. Quickly, he opened the bag and pulled up the mirror.

Then he held the mirror against the window and shouted "Come on in! I'll put you in the bag too!"

The cousin took one look at the ghost in the bag and floated off as fast as he could go.

From that time on Tom lived in peace. He was clever enough to keep his bag of barber tools handy, although he never had to use them again.

Baba Yaga
A Russian witch story

Who is Baba Yaga? She is a witch! There are many Russian fairy tales about her. Here is one for you to read.

Baba Yaga lives in a little house that stands on chicken legs. When she wants to travel, she sits in a *mortar* and pushes it along with a *pestle*. She uses a broom to sweep her tracks away.

Baba Yaga has iron teeth, and she often eats children! Well, that is what the fairy tales say...

I N a little house in the country lived an old man and his little girl. The little girl's mother had died long ago. And now the old man decided he should get married again.

"Then you will have a new mother," he told the little girl. "You will have a good woman to take care of you."

But the new wife was not a good woman. She was mean to the little girl and made her work very hard.

She made her sweep dust from the road in the summertime. She made her sweep snow from the road in winter. But no matter how mean the old woman was, the little girl was always cheerful.

The old woman simply hated the little girl. "I must get rid of her somehow," she thought.

One morning, when the little girl's father had gone to take some wheat to market, the old woman said to the little girl: "If you will go to your good aunt, my sister, and ask her for a needle and thread, I will make you a dress."

The little girl put her pretty red kerchief over her head and set off.

On the way, she thought to herself, "I have a good aunt, it is true. But she is not my stepmother's sister. My *good* aunt is my *real* mother's sister. I will go to her first and ask her what I should do."

The little girl's aunt was happy to see her.

"Aunty," said the little girl, "my father's wife wants me to go to her sister to ask for a needle and thread to sew me a dress. But first I have come to ask you what I should do."

"It's a good thing you came to me first," said the aunt. "Your stepmother's sister is none other than Baba Yaga, the cruel witch.

"But I can help you. Take
this ribbon,
this can full of oil,
this loaf of fresh bread,
this, ham.

"Now listen to me: In Baba Yaga's garden there is a birch tree that will try to whip you with its branches. You must tie this pretty ribbon around its trunk.

"You will see a big gate that creaks. It will try to lock you in. You must pour this oil on its hinges.

"You will see some hungry dogs. They will want to eat you. Throw them the bread.

"And you will meet a cat who could scratch your eyes out. Give the ham to the cat.

"Because you are so brave and so good, you will be stronger than all the wicked creatures you may meet."

The little girl thanked her good aunt and set off.

She walked and she walked and she kept on walking. At last she came to the house of the old witch, Baba Yaga.

Baba Yaga was sitting in front of an embroidery frame embroidering.

"Good morning, aunt."

"Good morning, child."

"Your sister wants a needle and thread so she can make me a dress," said the little girl.

"Very well," said the witch, "I will look for some thread and for a needle that is good and sharp. While you are waiting for me, you can sit here at the embroidery frame and embroider."

The little girl sat down to embroider.

Baba Yaga had embroidered a very pretty red and yellow flower with silk thread.

"You are so pretty," said the little girl to the flower. "What are you doing in the house of an old witch?"

"I am a prisoner," said the flower. "Will you set me free?"

"I would like to set you free," said the little girl, "but I don't know what to do."

"Just take the stitches out carefully," said the flower. "Take them out one by one."

Carefully, carefully, the little girl began to take out the stitches with her needle.

"Gently . . . gently . . ." said the flower.

At last there was nothing left on the embroidery frame but the outline of the flower marked by little needle holes.

Suddenly the little girl heard Baba Yaga talking to the cook in the courtyard. "Heat

some water for a bath and wash my niece carefully. I am going to eat her for dinner."

The little girl shook with fear as she watched the cook bring in wood for the fire and pails of water for the bath. But she tried to sound cheerful. "You are working too hard!" she said to the cook. "It would be easier if you chopped less wood and carried the water in a sieve."

The cook burst out laughing and said, "You are right! And what a pretty red kerchief you are wearing!"

"It is for you," said the little girl.

"Thank you! Thank you!" said the cook. And she ran to put the kerchief away.

The little girl looked around the room. The fire in the fireplace began to burn brightly. The water began to boil in the pot. The little girl thought, "If I were visiting my good aunt right now, she would make me a glass of tea and give me a slice of bread and butter."

Meanwhile, the old witch Baba Yaga was waiting in the courtyard. She called, "Are you embroidering, child?"

"I am embroidering, aunt, I am embroidering."

Then, quietly, quietly, the little girl got up and crept to the door — but there was the cat looking hungry and mean! His green eyes stared into the blue eyes of the little girl. He spread out his claws to scratch her.

But the little girl gave the ham to the cat and whispered, "Tell me, I beg of you, how can I get away from Baba Yaga?"

First the cat ate all the ham. Then he licked his whiskers. Then he answered.

"See this comb and this towel? Take them

and run. Baba Yaga will come after you, so you must listen for her. Put your ear to the ground. When you hear her coming, throw the towel down — and you will see what happens!

"Then," the cat went on, "put your ear to the ground again and if you hear Baba Yaga coming again, throw down the comb — and you will see what happens!"

The little girl thanked the cat, took the towel and the comb, and ran out of the house.

But just outside she saw two dogs — they looked even hungrier and meaner than the cat. They were about to eat her up. She threw them the fresh bread her aunt had given her, and they did her no harm.

Next she came to the big gate that creaked and wanted to lock her in. But the clever little girl poured the whole can of oil on its hinges, and the gate opened wide.

Outside the gate the birch tree tried to whip the little girl with its branches. But she tied a red ribbon around its trunk. Then the birch tree bowed to the little girl and pointed to the road. The little girl ran and ran and kept on running.

Meanwhile, the cat sat in front of the embroidery frame and began to embroider.

From the courtyard the old witch Baba Yaga called again, "Are you embroidering, child? Are you embroidering?"

"I am embroidering, old witch, I am embroidering," the cat said in a very impolite voice.

Baba Yaga stamped her foot and rushed into the house. The little girl was gone! She ran to the embroidery frame. The pretty flower was gone! In its place the cat had embroidered a mouse's tail!

Baba Yaga beat the cat with a stick and cried, "Why didn't you scratch her eyes out?"

"Well," said the cat, "I've been working for you for many years, and you have never given me even the smallest bone. But the little girl gave me a ham!"

Baba Yaga beat the dogs with her stick. "Why did you let her get away?"

"Well," said the dogs, "we have been working for you for many years, and what did you ever give us? Not even a little piece of dry bread! But the little girl gave us a big loaf of fresh bread."

Baba Yaga kicked the big gate. "Why?" she said. "Why? Why?"

"Well," said the gate, "I have been working for you for many years, and you have never put one drop of oil on my hinges. But the little girl poured a whole can of oil over them."

Baba Yaga scolded the birch tree. "Well," said the tree, "I have been working for you for

many years, and you have never decorated me even with a thread. But the little girl tied a beautiful silk ribbon around my trunk."

"And I," said the cook — although no one had said a word to her — "ever since I began working for you, you have never given me even a rag. But the little girl gave me a pretty red kerchief."

The cook had to climb the cherry tree to get away from angry Baba Yaga.

"Just you wait," cried Baba Yaga. "I will catch the little girl and eat her in spite of all of you. And don't be so proud of your red kerchief!" she said to the cook. "Tomorrow I will sell it to the gypsy!"

Red with rage, Baba Yaga grabbed a broom and her pestle and jumped into her mortar. She rushed across the country, using the pestle to push herself along and sweeping away her tracks with a broom.

But the little girl had her ear to the ground. She could hear Baba Yaga getting closer.

She threw the towel down. And behold! The towel became a big river. Baba Yaga had to stop. She ground her iron teeth together and rolled her yellow eyes.

Then she ran to the house and got three oxen and led them to the river. The oxen drank up all the river — to the very last drop. And Baba Yaga jumped into the mortar and went after the little girl again.

The little girl was far away by now. She stopped to put her ear to the ground, and she heard the sound of the mortar on the road. Quickly she threw the comb behind her, and behold! The comb became a forest of pine trees.

Baba Yaga tried to get through the forest. Impossible!

She tried to cut down the pine trees with her iron teeth, but she broke all her teeth so that she could never again eat little children — or even chicken!

The little girl listened again. She did not hear a thing — only the wind blowing through the forest. She kept on running very fast because it was getting dark. "My father will think I am lost," she thought.

When her father came back from the market, he asked his wife, "Where is my little girl?"

"Who knows?" replied the woman. "I sent her to her aunt's house on an errand three hours ago. Maybe she went to the woods to pick blackberries. Or maybe she went to play hopscotch with her friends."

"What a funny idea!" said the old man. "There are no blackberries in the woods at this time of year. And it is getting too dark to play hopscotch."

At last the little girl came running into the
house.

"Where have you been, my darling?" her
father asked.

"Oh dear papa," she said. "Your wife sent
me to her sister's house to get a needle and

thread to make me a dress. But her sister —
just imagine — is Baba Yaga, the cruel witch!"

And she told her father everything that had
happened.

The man's wife, who was
hiding behind the stove,
heard the little girl.

When she saw how angry the little girl's father was, the wife was so frightened that she ran away. She ran far, far away, and no one ever saw her again.

Since that time, the little girl and her father live in peace. I have been to their house. They invited me to eat with them. The tablecloth was very white, the cakes very fresh, and they were very happy.

The Goblin and the Tailor

A YOUNG BOY named Jack was sitting in his tailor shop, minding his own business — which was making jackets and trousers for the farmers who lived nearby.

Jack was working away quietly. His needle was going in and out, in and out, when all of a sudden the door banged open. In came a big man.

"My name is Macdonald," he said in a loud voice.

"Yes, I know," said Jack. "Everyone knows Macdonald, the richest landowner in Scotland."

"I'm looking for a tailor," said Macdonald.

"You're looking AT a tailor," said Jack.

"You? A tailor?" said Macdonald. "You're too young to be a tailor. Why, you're just a lad. Who taught you to sew?"

"My father taught me to sew," said Jack. "He taught me to be the best tailor in Scotland. The best and the bravest."

"The best?" said Macdonald. "We will soon see about that. I want a pair of trousers made of this velvet cloth. Can you cut them out, sew them up, and bring them to me tomorrow morning? Bring them to my castle at Saddell."

"Tomorrow morning," said Jack, "you will have the finest trousers in Scotland."

Jack measured the rich man. Then he sat up all night cutting and sewing. And in the morning he knocked at the castle gate and brought Macdonald a fine pair of trousers.

Macdonald tried on the trousers and looked in the mirror. "Perfect," he said.

"Yes, I know," said Jack. "My father taught me to sew. He taught me to be the best tailor in Scotland. The best and the bravest."

"The bravest?" said Macdonald. "We will soon see about that. I need a new jacket to go with these trousers. Now I dare you to make it tonight — in the graveyard."

"Do you mean that old graveyard on top of the hill?" asked Jack. "People say it is haunted by goblins and monsters!"

"So it is," said Macdonald. "And if you will sit there tonight till you finish my jacket, I will give you a big bag of gold. And I'll know that you are the best tailor in Scotland. The best and the bravest."

"And what if a goblin gobbles me up? What if a monster drags me under?" said Jack.

"Then I'll have to look for another tailor," said Macdonald.

When night came, away went Jack the tailor to the top of the hill — about half a mile from the castle. When he came to the old graveyard, Jack chose a big flat gravestone to sit on. He lighted his candle. He put on his thimble. And he set to work on the jacket. In and out went his needle. And all the time he was thinking of the big bag of gold Macdonald would give him.

Listen! What was that?

All of a sudden, Jack feels the ground shaking under his feet. He looks all about him, but he keeps on sewing. In and out goes his needle. And there, just behind him, a great ugly head is sticking out of the ground.

From the head comes a deep voice saying, **"Do you see this great head of mine?"**

"I see that, but I'll sew this," says Jack. And he sews away at the jacket. In and out goes his needle. In and out.

Now the ugly head sticks up higher until its neck is showing above the ground.

The deep voice speaks again. **"Do you see this great neck of mine?"**

"I see that, but I'll sew this," says Jack. And he sews away at the jacket.

Now the head and neck come up higher still, until the goblin's great shoulders and chest are above the ground. The deep voice says (and it sounds as loud as thunder): **"Do you see this great chest of mine?"**

"I see that, but I'll sew this," says Jack. In and out goes his needle. In and out.

And still the great goblin keeps coming through the ground, higher and higher. Now he shakes a great pair of arms in Jack's face. **"Do you see these great arms of mine?"**

"I see that, but I'll sew this," says Jack. In and out goes his needle. In and out. Jack has no time to waste. He begins taking bigger stitches.

While Jack the tailor is making his stitches bigger, he sees the great goblin coming out of the ground, slowly, slowly. Now it lifts out a great leg. The goblin stamps its leg on the ground and says in a roaring voice: **"Do you see this great leg of mine?"**

"Yes, yes! I see that, but I'll sew this!" cries Jack. And he begins sewing so fast and taking such big stitches that he is just finishing the jacket when the goblin begins to pull its other

leg out of the ground. But before it can get its foot out, Jack has finished the jacket. Jack blows out his candle, jumps down from the grave-stone, and runs out of the graveyard with the jacket under his arm.

The goblin gives a loud roar. He stamps his great feet and runs after Jack.

Down the hill they run, both of them. But Jack has a head start. And when he thinks of that big bag of gold, he runs even faster.

At last he reaches the castle. Jack runs inside the castle gate and slams it shut. Just in time too! Here comes the great goblin! Roaring with anger, he strikes the wall above the gate and leaves the mark of his five great fingers. You can see them to this day if you look close enough.

But that is all you will see of the goblin. For he went away and was never seen again.

As for Jack the tailor, he got his big bag of gold. And from that day on, the rich landowner Macdonald had all his clothes made by the best tailor in Scotland.

The best and the bravest.

Sources

"The Ghost Catcher" is based on "The Ghost Who Was Afraid of Being Bagged," a story from *Folk Tales of Bengal* by Lālavihārī De, published by Macmillan, London, 1883.

"Baba Yaga" is translated and adapted by permission of Flammarion et Cie from BABA YAGA (a "Père Castor" book), retold by Rose Celli, copyright 1932 by Ernest Flammarion, Paris.

"The Goblin and the Tailor" is based on "The Sprightly Tailor," in Joseph Jacobs' collection, *Celtic Fairy Tales* published by David Nutt, London, 1892.